W9-BLW-996

Lineberger Memorial
Library
Lutheran Theological Southern Seminary Columbia, S. C.

Copyright © 2001 by Chinlun Lee
All rights reserved.

First U.S. edition 2001
Library of Congress Cataloging-in-Publication Data
Lee, Chinlun.
The very kind rich lady and her one hundred dogs / Chinlun Lee. — 1st U.S. ed.
p. cm.

Summary: Every day the very kind rich lady feeds, cares for, and plays with her 100 dogs, some with plain names and some with fancy names.

ISBN 0-7636-1290-1
[1. Dogs — Fiction. 2. Pets — Fiction.] I. Title.
PZ7.L51188 Ve 2001 [E] — dc21 00-056424
2 4 6 8 10 9 7 5 3 1
Printed in Hong Kong
This book was typeset in American Typewriter. The illustrations were done in watercolor, ink, and pencil.
Candlewick Press, 2067 Massachusetts Avenue, Cambridge, Massachusetts 02140

THE
VERY KIND
RICH LADY AND HER
ONE HUNDRED DOGS
Chinlun Lee

Once there was a very kind rich lady who adopted one hundred stray dogs.

They all lived together in a tall house on a hill.

The very kind rich lady loved
her dogs very much.
There was . . .

Papa.

(That's one.)

There were . . .

Mr. Samuel

and **Mary.**

(That's three.)

There were . . .

Mrs. Fifi

and her four pups —

Eeny,

Meeny,

Miney,

and Mo.

(That's eight.)

There were . . .

Sooty,

Willow,

Coco,

Muffin,

Wesley J.,

Camel,

Yogurt,

Pudding,

Lola,

and Lady.

(That's eighteen.)

There were . . .
Honey,
Queenie,
Max,
Pepper,
Pirate,
Olive,
Julio,

Pizza,

Madeleine,

Candy,

Nero,

Pipi,

Nana,

Flint,

Mrs. Chips,

Ruthie,

and Tuesday.

(That's thirty-five.)

There were . . .

Ginger,

Abdul,

Pooch,

Jacket,

Tinkle,

Tammy,

Biscuit,

Toot,

Crystal,

Poppy,

Arthur,

Tangle,

Fluff,

Pretzel,

Esme,
Henry,
Molly,
Nova,
Scamp,
Buster,
Billy,
Toast,
Floss,
Morris,
Foxy,
and
Peanut.
(That's sixty-one.)

There were . . .
Crispin,
Jasmine,
Jumbo,
Scat,
Tara,
Juno,
Wags,
Yum-Yum,
Pig,
Zaba,
Archie,
Rusty,
Darling,
Moff,
Brutus,

Denver,
Sausage,
Spider,
Charlotte,
Princess,
Curry,
Smoky,
Silk,
Ruby,
Dizzy,
Harvey,
Hobo,
Captain,
Taffy,
Heidi,
Mountain,
Hank,
Chico,
Harpo,
Groucho,
Daisy,
Freddy,
and Mr. Scratch.
(That's ninety-nine.)

And Bingo,

who was always late.

Every day the lady
brushed her dogs
(at least ten
strokes each)

and searched their
coats for fleas.
(She found at least
one flea each.)

Then she
fed her dogs on
one hundred plates,

and fussed
over them,

and
talked to them,

and called them by

their one hundred names . . .

Papa, Meeny, Miney, Mo, Sooty, Willow, Coco, Pudding, Lola, Lady, Honey, Queenie, Julio, Pizza, Madeleine, Candy, Nero, Ruthie, Tuesday, Ginger, Abdul, Toot, Crystal, Poppy, Tammy, Henry, Molly, Nova, Scamp, Buster, Billy, Crispin, Jasmine, Jumbo, Tara, Juno, Scat, Wags, Darling, Brutus, Sausage, Denver, Ruby, Dizzy, Hobo, Harvey, Groucho, Harpo, Chico,

Mr. Samuel, Mary, Mrs. Fifi, Eeny,
Muffin, Wesley J., Camel, Yogurt,
Max, Pepper, Pirate, Olive,
Pipi, Nana, Flint, Mrs. Chips,
Pooch, Jacket, Tinkle, Biscuit,
Arthur, Tangle, Fluff, Pretzel, Esme,
Toast, Floss, Morris, Foxy, Peanut,
Pig, Yum-yum, Rusty, Archie, Zaba, Moff,
Princess, Spider, Curry, Charlotte, Smoky, Silk,
Taffy, Captain, Mountain, Heidi, Hank,
Daisy, Freddy, Mr. Scratch, and Bingo!

to come and play

with her on the hill.

And they did.

Even Bingo,

who was always late.

Did the very kind rich lady and
her dogs have a lovely
time together?

Woof!
Woof!
woof!
Wooof!
woof!
woof!
woof!
woof!
Woof!
woof!
woof!
woof!
Woof!
Woof!
woof!
woof!
WOOF!
Woooof!
Woof!
Yes!
Wooooof!
Woof!
Woof!
woof!
woof!
Woof!
wooof!
woooof!
woof!
woof!
Woof!
woof!
woof!
Woof!
Woof!
woof!
Woof!
Woof!
Woof!
Woof!
WOOF!
Woof!
Woof!
woof!
woof!
Woof!
woof!
woof!
Woof!
Woof!
Woof!
Woof!
Woof!
Woof!
woof!
WOOF!
Woof!

And every night
they all went home to bed.

Goodnight,
very kind rich lady.

Goodnight,

one hundred dogs.

PZ 7 .L51188 Ve 2001
Lee, Chinlun.
The very kind rich lady and
her one hundred dogs

LINEBERGER
MEMORIAL LIBRARY
LUTHERAN THEOLOGICAL
SOUTHERN SEMINARY
COLUMBIA, SOUTH CAROLINA 29203

DEMCO